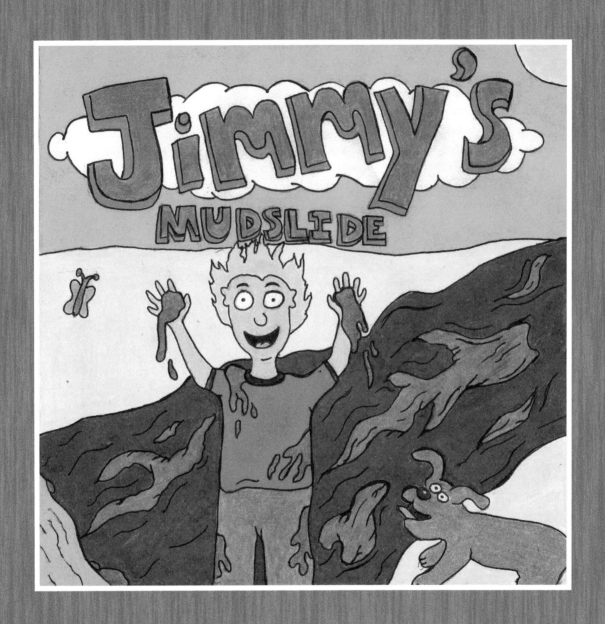

Jimmy's MUDSLIDE

Helene Vandeloo

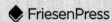

FriesenPress

Suite 300 - 990 Fort St
Victoria, BC, V8V 3K2
Canada

www.friesenpress.com

ISBN
978-1-5255-7462-7 (Hardcover)
978-1-5255-7463-4 (Paperback)
978-1-5255-7464-1 (eBook)

1. JUVENILE FICTION, IMAGINATION & PLAY

Distributed to the trade by The Ingram Book Company

 DEDICATION

My adventure began when I grew up with a younger brother, Paul, and then when I raised two sons, Chris and Nick.

I fondly remember my sons coming into the house covered in dirt, leaves, mud, and anything else you could find on the ground or up a tree.

This is what inspired this story about *Jimmy's Mudslide* — it's a piece of my heart.

This story is dedicated to my amazing sons, Christopher and Nicholas.

Rain, rain, rain. It had been raining steadily for three days. It was the start of the summer holidays and Jimmy was stuck inside the house. Jimmy was very restless and bored. He was tired of playing cards and board games with his mother and his older sister, Gracie. He was tired of playing his video game box. Jimmy just wanted to get outside to play.

Jimmy woke up on the fourth day and the sun was shining brightly.

"Yeah!" Jimmy shouted. He put on his ragged jeans, a T-shirt, socks, and his running shoes. He dashed downstairs to go out the side door when his mom hollered, "Jimmy, sit down and eat your breakfast!"

"Aw, Mom," Jimmy moaned. He sat at the table and ate a bowl of cereal and drank his orange juice. He took his vitamin and jumped from his chair to head outside.

"Put your rubber boots on, Jimmy. The ground is very wet and soggy after all the rain we've had. Don't get too muddy! Oh, and don't forget, I'm having the book club meeting here this morning," said Mom.

Jimmy quickly changed into his boots and ran outside with his dog Spike. He picked up his pail and small fishing net. He looked at Spike and said, "Let's see how many minnows we can catch today."

Jimmy ran into the backyard. He stopped at the edge of a small hill. The hill sloped down towards the shallow creek. *Whoosh!* The ground gave way and Jimmy was sliding down the hill. He hit the creek and laughed and laughed. Jimmy was covered in mud. His hair was slimy, his T-shirt was muddy, and his jeans were mucky.

"That was great!" Jimmy shouted. He scrabbled up the other side of the hill and went down the slide again.

His friend Brian, who lived next door, climbed over the fence and ran into the backyard. He saw Jimmy and started to laugh, and then, *Whoosh!* Brian was downhill in the mud. He landed in the creek and screeched, "That was awesome!"

Jimmy and Brian were hooting and hollering very loudly. Other kids in the neighbourhood raced into Jimmy's backyard to see why it was so noisy. Jeff, Dane, and Sam saw Jimmy and Brian all covered in mud and started to laugh. The three boys were standing at the edge of the hill when suddenly they were all sliding in the mud down to the creek. They scrambled up the side of the hill and shouted, "Let's do it again!" Laughing and shouting, the five boys went for another ride down the muddy hill. They climbed back up and looked at each other and shrills of laughter could be heard around the neighbourhood.

"We're the Mudmen!" Jimmy shrieked. "I think I got mud up my nose on the last slide."

Jimmy's mom stood on the back deck with a stern look on her face. Other moms joined her. They were all looking at the filthy, yucky, ghastly sight of their boys. Jimmy looked up and saw his mom and grinned. "Uh, hi, Mom. I was just trying to catch some minnows."

All the moms on the back deck were laughing hysterically.

"Well," said Mom. "We did want to get them out of the house."

ABOUT THE AUTHOR

Jimmy's Mudslide follows Helene Vandeloo's debut novel, *Gracie's Wheels*. *Jimmy's Mudslide* is a continuation of Helene's desire to help young readers find joy in reading, and reminds them that they can also have adventures that lead to unforgettable stories.

CPSIA information can be obtained
at www.ICGtesting.com
Printed in the USA
BVHW050744091120
592842BV00013B/688